The High Hills

For Peter

Library of Congress Cataloging-in-Publication Data

Barklem, Jill.
  The high hills.

  Summary: Inspired by an old tale, young mouse
Wilfred uses a trip into the hills as an opportunity
to look for gold and explore unknown country.
  [1. Mice—Fiction.   2. Explorers—Fiction.
3. Adventure and adventurers—Fiction]   I. Title.
PZ7.B25058Hi   1986   [E]   86–8177
ISBN 0–399–21361–9

Text and illustrations copyright © 1986 by Jill Barklem.
First published in the United States 1986 by
Philomel Books,
a division of The Putnam Publishing Group,
51 Madison Avenue, New York, N.Y. 10010
First impression

Printed in Great Britain by
William Collins Sons & Co. Ltd.
Glasgow.

The High Hills

JILL BARKLEM

PHILOMEL BOOKS

It was the very end of autumn. The weather was damp and chilly and Wilfred was spending the day inside with the weavers. *Clickety, clack* went the loom, *whirr, whirr* went the spinning wheel. Lily and Flax were in a hurry.

"We must finish in time," said Flax. "We promised Mr. Apple."

"What are you making?" asked Wilfred.

"Blankets," replied Lily.

"Who are they for?" said Wilfred.

"They are for the voles in the High Hills," replied Flax. "They have just discovered that the moths have eaten all their quilts and they've no time to make new ones before the cold weather comes. They're too busy gathering stores for winter. We're helping out."

"Can I help too?" asked Wilfred.

"That's kind of you, Wilfred, but not just now," said Lily. "Why don't you find yourself a book to read while I finish spinning this wool?"

Wilfred went over to the bookcase. On a shelf, tucked between volumes on dyestuffs and weaves, he found a thick book called *Daring Explorers of Old Hedge Days*. He settled himself comfortably and began to turn the pages.

"Sir Hogweed Horehound," he read, "determined to conquer the highest peak of the High Hills, for there, he knew, he would discover gold. Alone he set forth, taking in his trusty pack all he needed to survive the rigorous journey . . ."

Wilfred sat entranced. The whirr of the spinning wheel became the swish of eagles' wings, the clatter of the loom, the sound of falling rock, and the drops of rain on the window, jewels from the depths of some forgotten cave. Was there really gold in the hills beyond Brambly Hedge, he wondered.

Suddenly a door slammed. It was his mother come to fetch him home for tea.

"I hope he hasn't been too much trouble," said Mrs. Toadflax.

"He has been so quiet, we'd almost forgotten he was here," said Lily. "You can send him down again tomorrow if you like."

Lily and Flax were already hard at work when Wilfred arrived the next morning. He settled down by the window again to read about Sir Hogweed Horehound and his intrepid search for gold.

The morning flew past and by the time Mr. Apple arrived to collect Wilfred, Flax and Lily had almost finished the cloth.

"I'm sorry we couldn't match the yellow," said Flax. "We've used the last of Grandpa Blackthorn's lichen and no other dye will do."

"Never mind," said Mr. Apple. "It's the blankets they need. We'll take them up to the hills tomorrow."

"The hills," repeated Wilfred. "Are you really going up to the High Hills?"

"Yes," replied Mr. Apple. "Why?"

"Can I come?" Wilfred asked desperately. "Please say I can."

"Oh, I don't think so," said Mr. Apple. "It's too far. We shall have to stay overnight."

"I'll be very good," urged Wilfred.

Mr. Apple relented. "We'll see if your mother agrees," he said. "Come on, young mouse. It's time to go home."

To Wilfred's surprise, his mother did agree.

"It will do him good to be in the open air," she said. Wilfred rushed upstairs to pack. He knew just what he would need. Sir Hogweed Horehound had listed all the essential gear in his book: rope, a whistle, food, firesticks,

cooking pots, a groundsheet and blankets, a spoon, a water bottle and a first-aid kit.

"And I had better have a special bag for the gold," said Wilfred to himself as he gathered everything together.

He went to bed straight after supper. It was a long way to the High Hills and to get to the Voles' Hole by dusk, they would have to make an early start.

Next morning, soon after dawn, Flax, Lily and Mr. Apple called for Wilfred. They were carrying packs on their backs, full of cloth and blankets, and there was honey and cheese and a pudding for the voles from Mrs. Apple. Wilfred hurried down the stairs.

"Whatever have you got there?" asked Flax.

"It's my essential gear," explained Wilfred.

"You won't be needing a cooking pot. I've got some sandwiches," said Mr. Apple.

"But I must take everything," said Wilfred. His lip began to quiver. "How can I find gold without my equipment?"

"You'll have to carry it then," said Mr. Apple. "We can't manage any more."

The first part of the journey was easy. The four mice went up the hedge, past Crabapple Cottage, the Store Stump and Old Oak Palace. Then they rounded the weavers' cottages and arrived at the bank of the stream. Carefully they picked their way over the stepping stones and clambered up into the buttercup meadow.

Wilfred strode through the grass, occasionally lifting his paw to gaze at the distant peaks. Beyond the bluebell woods he could see the path begin to climb.

Mr. Apple looked back. "How's my young explorer?" he said. "Ready for lunch?"

"Oh, please," said Wilfred, easing off his pack with relief.

The mice ate their picnic and enjoyed the late autumn sunshine but soon it was time to go on. All through the afternoon they walked. The path became steeper and steeper, and when they looked behind them, they could see the fields and woods and hedges spread out far below.

By tea-time, it was getting dark and cold,
and the hills around were shrouded in mist.
At last they saw a tiny light shining from a rock
beneath an old hawthorn tree.

"Here we are," said Mr. Apple. "Knock on
the door, Wilfred, will you?"

An elderly vole opened it a crack. When
she saw Mr. Apple, she cried, "Pip! Fancy you
climbing all this way, and with your bad leg
too. Come in, do."

"We couldn't leave you without blankets,
now could we," said Mr. Apple.

The mice crowded into the cottage and were
soon sitting round the fire, drinking hot
bilberry soup and resting their weary paws.

For Wilfred, the conversation came and went
in drifts and soon he was fast asleep. Someone
lifted him gently onto a little bracken bed in
the corner and the next thing he knew was the
delicious smell of breakfast, sizzling on the range.

Wilfred ate heartily, oatcakes with rowanberry jelly, and listened to the voles describing their hard life in the hills. He was disappointed when Mr. Apple announced that it was time to leave.

"Can't we explore a bit first?" he begged.

"Flax and I have to get back to work," said Lily, "but why don't you two follow on later?"

"Well," relented Mr. Apple, "there are some fine junipers beyond the crag . . ."

"And Mrs. Apple *loves* junipers," said Wilfred quickly, "let's get her some."

So the mice said goodbye to the voles and Mr. Apple and Wilfred set off up the winding path.

Wilfred ran on ahead and was soon round the crag. When Mr. Apple caught up with him, Wilfred was half way up a steep face of rock.

"Wilfred!" cried Mr. Apple. "Come down."

"Just a minute," shouted Wilfred. "I've found something."

Mr. Apple watched as Wilfred pulled himself
up onto the narrow ledge and started scraping
at the rock and stuffing something in his pocket.

"Look!" cried Wilfred. "Gold!"

"Don't be silly, Wilfred," shouted Mr. Apple.
"That's not gold. Come down at once."

Wilfred looked over the side. His voice faltered.
"I can't," he said. "I'm scared."

Mr. Apple was exasperated. "Wait there," he
shouted. Slowly he climbed the steep rocks,
carefully placing his paws in the clefts of the
stones. The ledge was very narrow. "We'll
edge along this way. Perhaps the two paths

will meet," he said. "We certainly can't go down the way we came up."

As they walked cautiously along the ledge, an ominous mist began to rise from the valley.

"If only we had some rope," said Mr. Apple. "We ought to rope ourselves together."

Wilfred put his paw in his pack and produced the rope! Mr. Apple tied it carefully round

Wilfred's middle and then round his own. And it was just as well for a few minutes later they were engulfed in a thick white fog.

"Turn to the rock face, Wilfred, we'll ease our way along, one step at a time."

They went on for a long time, then they took a rest. As they sat on the wet rock, the mist parted for a few seconds, just long enough to show a deep strange valley below.

Mr. Apple was worried. He had no idea where they were. It looked as though they would have to spend the night on the mountain. It would be very cold and dark, and all he had in his pocket were two sandwiches the voles had given him for the journey down. His leg was feeling stiff and sore too. What was to be done? He explained the situation to Wilfred.

"It's all my fault," said Wilfred, "I didn't mean us to get lost. I just wanted to find gold like Sir Hogweed."

"Never mind," said Mr. Apple. "We must look for somewhere to spend the night."

A short way along the path, the ledge became a little wider. Under an overhang of rock a small cave ran back into the mountainside.

"Look," cried Wilfred, slinging his pack inside. "Base camp!"

Mr. Apple sat gingerly on the damp moss at the mouth of the cave. Everything felt damp, his clothes, his whiskers, his handkerchief.

"I wish I'd brought my pipe, we could have made a fire," he sighed. "Never mind, we'll huddle close and try to keep warm."

But Wilfred was busily searching in his pack again. Out came the firesticks and the tinderbox. "I'll see if there's some dry wood at the back of the cave," he said enthusiastically.

"Wilfred," cried Mr. Apple in admiration, "you're a real explorer."

Soon they had a cheerful blaze on the ledge outside the cave. Wilfred produced two blankets and the mice wrapped themselves up snugly while their clothes dried in front of the fire. The little kettle was filled from the water bottle and proudly Wilfred set out a feast of bread and cheese and honeycakes.

"You know," said Mr. Apple, as he settled back against the rock. "I haven't enjoyed a meal so much for years."

To while away the time, Mr. Apple began to tell Wilfred stories of his adventurous youth, and as they talked, the mists gradually cleared and a starry sky spread out above them. All was quiet but for the murmur of a stream which ran through the valley below like a silver ribbon in the moonlight. Warmed by the fire, they became drowsy and soon fell asleep.

The next morning they were woken by the sun shining into the cave.

"It's a beautiful day," called Wilfred, peering over the ledge, "and I can see a path down the mountain."

Mr. Apple sat up and stretched his leg. It still hurt. "We'll have to go down slowly, I'm afraid," he said.

"Is it your leg?" said Wilfred. "I can help," and he brought out a jar of comfrey ointment from his first-aid kit.

They packed up and set off down the path. Mr. Apple did the best he could but his leg was very painful. He managed to get as far as the stream but then he stopped and sat on a boulder with a sigh. "I can't go any further," he said. "What are we to do?"

The two mice sat in silence and watched the water swirl past the bank.

"Don't worry," said Wilfred, trying to be cheerful. "We'll think of something."

Suddenly he jumped up. "I've got it," he cried excitedly. "We'll *sail* down the stream!" He ran to the bank and with his ice-axe, he hooked out some large sticks that had caught behind a rock in the water. Using his rope to lash them together, he made a raft. "Come on," said Wilfred, "we'll shoot the rapids!"

"Are you sure this is a good idea?" said Mr. Apple. "Wherever will we end up?"

"Don't worry," said Wilfred. "It's all going to be all right."

Carefully they climbed onto the raft, Mr. Apple let go of the bank and they were off!

They were swept to the middle of the stream as it raced down the mountainside, twisting and turning, sweeping and splashing, careering over rocks and cutting through deep banks.

"My hat," shouted Wilfred. "I've lost my hat."

"Never mind that," cried Mr. Apple, "just hold on tight. There's a boulder ahead."

Wilfred gripped the sides of the raft, and somehow they managed to keep the raft, and themselves, afloat.

Down by the stream, Dusty was ferrying a
search party of mice over to the buttercup
meadows when he suddenly caught sight of a small
red hat floating along on the current.

"Look there," he shouted. All the mice peered
over the side of the boat.

"It's Wilfred's hat," cried out Mrs. Toadflax.
"Whatever can have happened to him?"

"Can Wilfred swim?" enquired Mrs. Apple
anxiously.

Meanwhile Wilfred and Mr. Apple were
beginning to enjoy their trip on the river. The
ground had levelled out and the pace of the
stream had become gentler. They looked about
them with interest.

"Wilfred," called Mr. Apple, "can you see what
I can see? I'm sure that's our willow ahead."

Wilfred stared at the bank. "It is!" he yelled.

"And there's the Old Oak Palace and the hornbeam. This is *our* stream!"

As they rounded the bend, they saw the Brambly Hedge mice climbing out of Dusty's boat. At the very same moment, Mrs. Apple looked up and cried, "Look! Look! There they are!"

The mice turned in amazement; the raft was almost abreast of them.

"Quick," shouted Dusty, "catch hold of this rope and I'll haul you to shore," and he tossed it to Wilfred.

As the two mice clambered out of the raft and up onto the bank, they all hugged each other.

"Wilfred, you're safe," cried Mrs. Toadflax.

"My dear, what has happened to your leg?" said Mrs. Apple.

Lord Woodmouse took charge. "Come on, everybody," he said. "Let's get these travellers home and dry, and then we can hear the full story."

The mice made their way along
the hedgerow to the hornbeam tree. Soon
everybody was sitting round the fire, eating cake
and drinking acorn coffee.

"Now tell us exactly what happened," urged Flax.

"Well, it was my fault," explained Wilfred again.
"I was looking for gold and I got stuck.
Mr. Apple had to rescue me and then we got
lost. And Mr. Apple's leg hurt so much, we had
to come back on the raft."

"Did you find any gold?" interrupted Primrose.

"No, only this silly old dust," said Wilfred, pulling
the bag out of his pocket. Flax and Lily gasped.

"Wilfred! That's not dust. That's Grandpa
Blackthorn's lichen. It's very rare. You *are* clever!
Wherever did you find it?"

Primrose ran to fetch some paper and Wilfred
proudly drew a map so that they could find the
place again.

"And when we go, you shall come with us,
Wilfred," promised Lily.

Mr. Apple was tired and soon he and Mrs. Apple went home to Crabapple Cottage. One by one, the visitors drifted away. It was time for the explorer to go to bed.

Wilfred followed his mother up the stairs.

"What adventures!" she said, washing his face and paws and helping him take off his muddy dungarees.

Wilfred climbed into bed. As his mother tucked him in, he thought of his night beneath the stars and snuggling down under his warm blankets, he was soon fast asleep.